Glam Girl

Get glamorous and create your own style
with over 30 fashion and craft ideas.

BARRON'S

by **DIANA KAPP** and **LIZ KRIEGER**
Illustrations by Shelly Meridith Delice

First edition for the United States and Canada published in 2003 exclusively by Barron's Educational Series, Inc.

Created and produced by Orange Avenue Publishing, San Francisco.

© 2003 by Orange Avenue Publishing

Illustrations © 2003 by Shelly Meridith Delice

Text © 2003 by Diana Kapp and Liz Krieger

All inquiries should be addressed to:
Barron's Educational Series, Inc.
250 Wireless Boulevard
Hauppauge, NY 11788
http://www.barronseduc.com

International Standard Book No. 0-7641-2290-8

Library of Congress Catalog Card No. 2002110407

Printed in China

9 8 7 6 5 4 3 2 1

credits:

Writers: **Diana Kapp and Liz Krieger**

Illustrator: **Shelly Meridith Delice**

Graphic Designers: **Madeleine Budnick and Kristine Mudd**

Editor: **Erin Conley**

Production Artists: **Doug Popovich**

Photography and Craft Makers: **Domini Dragoone and Airlie Anderson**

Art Directors: **Tanya Napier and Hallie Warshaw**

Created and Produced by Orange Avenue Publishing, San Francisco

Glam Girl

Table of contents

Decked out 8

Mascara Mane, page 24

Tressed out 20

Fab-u Flip-Flops, page 10

Heaven Scent,
page 34

And we **don't** mean not-a-hair-out-of-place coifs or perfectly polished toes and nails that match your belt and bag. Going glam is using ideas and inspirations to **spark** your natural beauty, making fashion less about brand names and more about **saucy** individual style, transforming a basic body scrub into a night of **pampering**, and revamping your hair hue to present the true you.

If you've **ever** wanted to fashion your own funky flip-flops, flaunt a faux mole, or personalize your lip balm and perfume, we've got activities, recipes, and do-it-now ideas worthy of the most discriminating style mavens. **Raid the pantry** for salon-grade face masks, critique each other's style quotient with glam slam books, and pilfer glam goods from your beau or your bro. From your dresses to your tresses, and even your stepping-out attitude, there are endless possibilities in these pages.

But this book is about way more than steppin' out in style. It's about getting together with best friends and bonding over secrets as you go beyond beauty to tap into what's uniquely you. This is the stuff of girldom, the best of what being a gal is about – no boys allowed here. We know you've got it – so flaunt it.

Go bold!
Go brazen!
Go glam!

Decked out

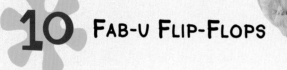

10 Fab-u Flip-Flops

11 Too-Cute Toe Rings

12 Cheapskate Glam

13 Trash-to-Treasure
Clothes Swap

fab-u flip-flops

What better way to show off that pretty pedi than by sporting a pair of fun and funky flip-flops? Make your own, and they'll be as unique as you are. Whether you're after sassy stripes or glittery glam, get crafty and strut those stylin' feet!

grab:

* 1 OR 2 PAIRS OF FLIP-FLOPS
* GLUE (A KIND THAT STICKS TO RUBBER)
* NEEDLE AND THREAD
* FABRIC PENS OR PAINTS
* A VARIETY OF FUN DECORATIONS
* THIN CRAFT WIRE

here's how:

* You're the designer, so get sketching! Lay out your flip-flops and decorations — and dream up a pair you'd love to wear.

* Test the glue. Attach a single bead or flower — and see that it sticks. Remove before it dries completely.

* Deck 'em out. These shoes are super easy and cheap, so make a pair for every mood! Draw designs with fabric paints or pens on the soles and straps. Stripes, dots, squiggles, and curlicues are all fun. For a mod look, try geometric squares and circles. Feeling patriotic? Show your stars and stripes.

the look:

Glam-o-Rama

Rhinestones, crystal beads, or glitter create shimmery style. Wrap shiny ribbon around the straps. Attach beads and stones one by one, or string some and glue them down.

Queen of Sheba

Glue gold and silver coins and trinkets to the straps. Create a flower out of coins and attach in the center. Add metallic polish to your toes, and you're an Egyptian princess for a day.

Flower Power

Embrace your tacky side – the faker the better is rule of thumb here. Attach a big floppy plastic flower in the center and fasten fun beads down the straps.

Fruity Tooty

Twist wire around bunches of plastic grapes and wind around the strap. Let a ladybug land in the corner.

Too-Cute Toe Rings

With flip-flops so fine, your toes are sure to attract extra attention. Why not deck them out in cool toe rings? The newest look: Clear elastic toe rings with a single jewel centerpiece.

To make your own: Find clear stretchy elastic at a craft shop. String a single sparkly bead and tie it around your toe.

Or if subtlety suits your style, string tiny strands of beads and wear three or four stacked up at a time.

cheapskate glam

While some gals say you can never be too rich or too thin, a true GlamGirl says pshaw to that petty thinking. Chic is an attitude and style comes cheap to those who just put a little sweet talk to work. We suggest pilfering goods from the closets of those close to you ... What's yours is mine is the mantra here!

Pilfered from	the item	making it your own
gram	MINK STOLE OR FAUX-FUR WRAP	WITH JEANS, TO GO COSMOPOLITAN CASUAL
	GAUDY, BIGGER-IS-BETTER RINGS	STRING AROUND YOUR NECK FOR A NEW LOOK
	CASHMERE CARDIGAN	OVER TANKS AND TEES FOR EVERYDAY
	VINTAGE PERFUME BOTTLES, PILL BOXES, OR VIALS	FILL WITH LIP BALM OR PERFUME
kid sis	TINY BOBBY PINS, PLASTIC BARRETTES, AND BUTTERFLY HAIR CLIPS	SEVERAL STACKED AT A TIME LOOK CUTE
	TEENY PURSES IN PATENT LEATHER, CLEAR PLASTIC, OR BEADED FABRIC	STYLISH STORAGE FOR LIPSTICK AND LUNCH MONEY
	BUBBLEGUM RINGS AND OTHER OVERSIZE PLASTIC RINGS	BEST WITH PINK, BLUE, OR PALE GREEN NAILS
beau	FLANNEL SHIRTS WORN TO PERFECTION	TIE UP IN A CENTER KNOT FOR A SASSY LOOK
	FADED OVERSIZE JEANS	ROLL-'EM, PATCH-'EM, BELT-'EM
	OLD-SCHOOL FELT BASEBALL HAT	BACKWARDS, BADGAL!
bro	PJ BOTTOMS IN COTTON OR FLANNEL	ROLL THEM TO CAPRI LENGTH AND WEAR WITH FITTED TEE OR SWEATER
	CLASSIC WHITE OXFORD (WITH CUFF LINKS FOR ADDED FUN)	WITH JEANS OR BLACK CIGARETTE PANTS
	LONG JOHNS (TOP AND BOTTOMS)	WITH A CASUAL SKIRT, TO MIX-UP THE LOOK

Trash-to-Treasure Clothes Swap

Who doesn't covet their best friend's clothes — those swingy suede bellbottoms and that to-die-for sequined top? Since "the grass is always greener" clearly applies to clothes, that fringed jeans skirt you think belongs nowhere but the garbage is likely to be the apple of your gal pal's eye. For a fun thrifty way to turn trash to treasure and spice up your style, hold a clothes swap!

here's how:

* Set aside an evening for swapping when your gang's all free. Make it festive with appetizers on tiny toothpicks and fun drinks under umbrellas.

* Tell everyone coming to clear their closets of reject clothes, shoes, and accessories — that means bringing anything that hasn't seen the light of day in a year. (Ask that everything be cleaned before the big night.)

* Set up chairs in a circle, and take turns show-and-telling clothes. Take time to tell stories the clothes have lived, like witnessing a killer kiss or supreme embarrassing moment.

* As each swapper presents her goods, let everyone claim what catches her fancy. Some GlamGirls follow the "if it fits, it's yours" rule; others take turns at first dibs. Whatever works, just play fair!

* Arrange for whatever is left over to get dropped off/picked up for donation to a local shelter or charity.

sixteen ways to tie a sarong

Twirl it into a turban, bind it into a bandeau, wrap it up as a sack. While formless fabric at first glance, a sarong can take most any shape, with some imagination. Whether your day demands a sun shield for your shoulders, a noontime nap mat, or a body-hugging halter, a sarong wears it well. Here are 16 surefire suggestions for assuring your sarong isn't shortchanged as "just a skirt"....

1
Tie up your belongings together on the end of a stick and run away Snoopy-style. Don't forget your travel snacks!

2 Cover up the rainbows and unicorns you painted on your bedroom wall when you were too young to know better.

3 Stash it in the trunk of your car for spur-of-the-moment picnics and stargazing.

4 Beat the boredom of a basic black sundress by tying it around your waist for a swingy skirt.

5 Hold it up to tune out Peeping Tom while putting on your bikini in the beach parking lot.

6 Fold in thirds the long way, tie tightly in back, and the sarong's a strapless bandeau. Knot in the front for another look.

7 Halve it, and show some knee by shortening it into a mini.

8 Twist it into a turban on a serious bad hair day.

9 Keep sunburn at bay with a "wear-ever" sun cover.

10 Wrap under your arms and tie in front, add strappy high heels, and you're perfect to go poolside at a hoity-toity resort.

11 Throw it on the seat of a sun-baked car to avoid a burned bum.

12 Crisscross and knot behind your neck, heap your hair high, and you're looking hot in a halter dress!

13 Sling up a pulled shoulder or achy elbow after a heated softball game.

14 Pile dirty clothes in it for a down-the-hall dash to the washer/dryer.

15 Snuggle underneath it on a long airplane trip.

16 Wrap around bare shoulders at the ceremony or formal part of an event; ditch it when the dancing starts!

All choked up

If you, like us, love candy necklaces, you're onto the charm of chokers. Whatever style you're looking to step out in — hippie chick or glittery glam — chokers help pull it off with pizzazz. Before you start, measure your neck so you'll know how long to make your choker.

charmed

Collect fun charms — a Greek evil eye, a dog tag, a single pearl, a Chinese symbol — and string onto leather or thin black cord. A single doodad in the center works best. A tiny perfume vial makes for a sweet romantic look.

All Tied Up

Tie a small colorful silk scarf tightly around your neck as a choker. Choose a color that flatters your face. Let excess fabric hang down your back, or hide it under your shirt.

Haight Street Hip

Hit fabric stores for scraps of suede or ultra-suede. Some of our fave earthy colors: red, olive, and brown. Cut a 1-inch wide strip, sew a button on one end, cut a slit into the other end, and you're set in simple suede.

Vintage Vixen

Black velvet ribbon makes for classic choker charm. Try different widths for different looks. A single vintage pin or button in front adds interest. Sew buttons onto ribbon, or attach with a pin glued to the button's back.

Silver Streak

String tiny silver beads onto clear dental floss or beading string. Attach a clasp. Tie on three or four strings at a time for a chunkier choker. Tie multiple strands in a knot at the center (or twist together) for a different look.

camisole chic

Camisole, tank, slip, undershirt, tankini — it's the ~~teeny~~ tee with more names than inches of fabric. And there are even more ways to wear one than words to describe it — under, over, layered, even all on its own. While simple suits some situations, other times demand some decking out.

grab:

* 2 OR 3 SIMPLE CAMISOLES
* A CREATIVE MIX OF DECORATIONS

here's how:

* Decide what look you're after, then sketch some ideas out on paper.

* If your camisoles are white, you might want to dye them fun colors. Pastel colors for home-dyed shirts tend to work best. Follow fabric dye instructions and let dry before decorating.

* A single iron-on decal makes for simple chic. Look for dragons, Chinese characters, serpents, and other interesting designs. Or, try flowers and hearts for a feminine feel.

* Another way to go is to sew ribbon, lace, or tiny beads around the neckline. Also, a simple border added to the bottom looks sweet.

* Keep it simple is a good rule of thumb for these tiny tops. They work best as basics to pair with funky skirts, shorts, and pants.

save face

Being a slave to fashion is a serious cash drain! A great way to find fun — even designer — duds on the cheap is to bid for them on eBay® (ebay.com). Most clothes go for a third of their retail price or less!

which is worse?

* FORGETTING YOUR BRA OR YOUR UNDIES?

* TRYING TOO HARD TO LOOK HIP OR HAVING NO CLUE HOW TO LOOK HIP?

* WHITE SEE-THROUGH PANTS AND CROCODILE UNDIES OR A WHITE SEE-THROUGH TEE AND A BLACK BRA?

* SANDALS WITH SOCKS OR TOE HAIRS PEEKING THROUGH OPEN-TOE SANDALS?

* BLACK SOCKS WITH WHITE SNEAKS OR RUNNING SHOES WITH A SKIRT?

22 Bad Hair Day Busters

24 Mascara Mane

25 Tress Rx

 **26** **HOME BREW HAIR COLOR**

Bad Hair Day Busters

Hot Cross Buns

Buns aren't just for the school librarian anymore. Funk up this simple do with sassy chopsticks to give your top knot some tao.

grab:

* An elastic band
* A handful of bobby pins
* A set of chopsticks (or, in a pinch, two sharpened pencils will do)

here's how:

* Pull your hair into a low ponytail and tie with an elastic band.
* Twirl the ponytail around itself into a bun.
* Secure with a bobby pin or two. Angle each chopstick through the bun, crisscrossing the sticks.
* If you're feeling extra-ornamental, spruce up your sticks beforehand by gluing an array of beads or crystals to the ends.

The Simple Slick Back

No time to wash your hair? Sick of the frizzies crimping your style? This cool clean bun — for shoulder-length or longer hair — is a great look on any day.

grab:

* Hair gel (optional) * A pick or comb * An elastic band
* Bobby pins * Hair spray

here's how:

* Dampen your do. If you like, goop it up with any good hair gel.
* Use a wide-tooth comb or pick to smooth and untangle your hair.
* Secure your hair in a firm (but not overly tight) ponytail with an elastic band.
* Twist your ponytail, loop it around the elastic, and secure with bobby pins.
* Spray liberally with hair spray. If you have bangs, slick them back, to the side, or spike 'em up. You can dress up your bun up by adding jeweled hairpins or funky barrettes on the side.

Okay, so you're running ten minutes late for school and your hair just won't cooperate. Your cowlick won't quit, your curls are kinky, and you've got bed-head going on in the back — it's time for some emergency hair help. Here are four bad hair day fixes, sure to banish even the worst tress distress.

grab:
* Bandanna   * Elastic bands   * Ribbons, beads, baubles

here's how:
* Starting with wet or dry hair, divide hair into a center part.
* Secure each section with an elastic. You can place the pigtails low or high.
* Jazz up your tails with bright ribbons (pink polka dots might just complete your look!) or colorful plastic baubles.
* Fold a square bandanna in half to make a triangle.
* Place the long edge at your hairline, triangle pointing back and down. Tie the two other points in a simple knot at the nape of your neck, and pull the pigtails back.

Pigtail-Bandanna combo
Embrace your inner kid with this fun flirty pigtails-and-dude-rag combination. (A great choice for staying dry and frizz-free on a rainy day.)

Mascara Mane

Want a quick **change** for your boring hairdo? Go blond for the day, sport blue streaks for math class, or add brown highlights for that hot date. Drop that box of hair dye, lose the frost-n-tip color, and grab a **magic** mascara wand instead!

grab:

* VARIOUS COLORS OF HAIR OR EYELASH MASCARA

Blushing Bride of Frankenstein

Using white or silver mascara, paint two thick streaks from your temples backward. Pile hair in a high bun and come alive!

Lush Leopard

Got short dark hair you want to spice up for the night? Using a yellow or golden tone, paint chunks all over your head in a spotted safari-inspired pattern. For a subtler look, just wave the wand over the layers that frame your face. Get ready to roar!

Green Goddess

Slick your hair back into a low pony. Grab a bright spring-y hue and drag it through your hair in stripes, from the root to tip.

Tress RX

Everything you need to get your hair shiny, healthy, and soft is probably already in your pantry or fridge. Forget expensive conditioning masks in fancy packaging and make this home remedy. Grab a gal pal, clear the bathroom, and get going!

grab follicle food

* 1/2 CUP OLIVE OIL

* 1/2 CUP VEGETABLE OIL

* 1/2 CUP HONEY

here's how

* Combine ingredients in a small saucepan and heat until just boiling.

* Remove immediately from heat and let cool.

* Pour into a plastic spray bottle and spritz on the ends of wet hair.

* Wrap a warm wet towel around hair and leave for 1 hour. Gab with girlfriends while sitting pretty.

* Shampoo the mixture out of your hair, rinse, and dry as usual.

Home Brew Hair color

Go Blond!

This recipe will help give blondes a sun-kissed glow and bring subtle highlights to brunettes. Use this treatment on a sunny day for best results.

grab:

* 3/4 cup boiling water
* 3 tablespoons fresh or dried chamomile flowers
* 2 tablespoons fresh or dried calendula flowers
* Juice from 3 large lemons
* Old T-shirt or towel (to drape over your shoulders)

here's how:

* Bring water to a boil.
* Pour boiling water over the flowers and let steep for 20 minutes.
* Strain infusion, saving the liquid.
* Add the lemon juice and mix well.
* Pour the mixture into a spray bottle and spritz on dry hair, dampening your entire do.
* Head outdoors and hit the sunshine for 1/2–4 hours, depending on how much time you have and how blond you want to be!
* As your hair dries, continue spritzing it with the mixture. Don't forget the sunblock.
* Rinse hair well with water and apply a good moisturizing conditioner.

There's no need to heap your hair with harsh chemicals or subject yourself to salon sticker shock to get hair that shines with bright fun color. These home-brewed hair color recipes (no worries, they wash right out) will lighten, brighten, and make the most of your natural hair color. Whether you're a blond, brunette, or redhead at heart, there's a hue for you!

grab:

* 1/2 cup dried sage
* 1 tablespoon dried rosemary leaves
* 2 cups water
* 2 tablespoons apple cider vinegar mixed with 1 quart water
* Old T-shirt or towel (to drape over your shoulders)

here's how:

* Add sage and rosemary leaves to the water and simmer over medium heat for about 1 hour.
* Cool the concoction to room temperature, then strain and keep the liquid.
* Pour liquid into a spray bottle.
* Apply to wet hair, coating hair thoroughly.
* Leave on for 30–60 minutes. (The longer you leave the mixture on, the deeper the color.)
* Rinse hair with water.
* Rinse again with the vinegar/water mixture.

Brunette Bombshell

Add chestnut hues to your locks with this brunette potion. Who says blondes have more fun?

More Home Brew Hair color

Red Alert

If you're already a redhead, this rinse will brighten your natural hue. For brunettes, the brew will bring out the red highlights in your hair. The acidity helps tighten hair cuticles, which boosts shine and enhances vibrancy. Since this treatment is quick and messy, we suggest doing it in the shower!

grab:

* Cranberry juice
* Juice of 2 lemons or limes

here's how:

* Mix several cups of cranberry juice with the lemon or lime juice.
* Pour into a spray bottle.
* Saturate dry hair with the mixture.
* Leave on for 2 minutes — longer for a more intense red.
* Shampoo and condition well.

grab:

* 2 cups water

* 2 orange pekoe or black tea bags

* 1 tablespoon each dried sage, rosemary, beet juice, ground cloves, and parsley

* 2 tablespoons sunflower oil

* Old T-shirt or towel (to drape over your shoulders)

here's how:

* In a small saucepan, bring water to a boil.

* Remove from heat, add tea bags, herbs, and cloves; let steep for 15 minutes.

* Remove tea bags and strain out herbs.

* Continue to cool to room temperature.

* Add juice and oil.

* Pour liquid into spray bottle.

* Spray the brew on your hair, combing through until hair is coated.

* Leave it on for about 5 minutes, then rinse thoroughly.

Darkness Visible

If you have dark hair and you've always wanted a richer (think Elvira) hue, try this potent punch.

GlamGirl QUIZ

What's Your True Hue?

Who said you had to live with the haircolor you were born with? Is your inner redhead dying to be let out? Is a blond buried deep inside? Hair color is something you can definitely change – every week if you like! Answer this quick quiz to figure out your personal hair palette.

 Take a peek inside your closet. What's the dominant theme?

A. Flowery flip-flops, hipster jeans, and belly-baring tops

B. Dark flowing skirts, edgy concert tees

C. Well-worn jeans, prairie tops, and comfy cashmere sweaters

D. Bright fuzzy sweaters, cool striped pants, anything with a great graphic

 Think quick: What flower speaks to you?

A. Daisy   C. Tulip

B. Red rose   D. Gerber daisy

know-it-all

The hair dryer was originally invented as a vacuum cleaner. It was just "reversed" for hair use.

Mostly Ds: You're a carrottop inside, girl! You light the room up with your spirit and aren't afraid to experiment with color.

Mostly Cs: You've got that earthy natural glow going on, and delicious multidimensional browns express your sweet, caring, and grounded spirit.

3 Shoe shopping means?

A. Snapping up several pairs of hot high heels

B. Picking up the latest dark platform shoes

C. Drooling over a pair of vintage cowboy boots

D. Testing out some funky new roller-skate shoes

4 Your favorite lipstick hues?

A. Shimmering, glistening pinks

B.. Deep, dark, sultry reds

C. Barely-there browns and nudes

D. Peachy, punch pinks and reds

save face

Run out of hairspray but need some quick chemical-free hair hold? Chop a lemon into 1/2 inch bits, add 2 cups water, and boil until 1/2 is left. Let cool, strain, and spray away!

which is worse?

✱ HAT-HEAD OR BED-HEAD?

✱ OVER-DYED HAIR OR FAKE TANNING?

✱ ORANGE HAIR OR GREEN HAIR?

✱ MULLET OR MOHAWK?

✱ DANDRUFF OR HEAD LICE?

answers

MOSTLY As: YOU'RE A BLOND AT HEART — CAREFREE, FLIRTY, AND FUN. WHETHER YOU'RE AU NATUREL OR A BOTTLE-BLOND, YOUR SPIRIT SPEAKS OF SUNNY DAYS AND BEACHY FUN.

MOSTLY Bs: YOUR URBAN EDGE SHOWS THROUGH IN ANYTHING YOU DO. DARK RICH BROWNS AND BLACKS SUIT YOU BEST AND STREET-INSPIRED FASHIONS, DARING HAIRDOS, AND FUNKY ACCESSORIES ARE YOUR THING.

 **34** HEAVEN SCENT

35 BOTTLE IT UP!

36 BODY ART

38 FAUX MOLES

39 SHIMMER GLIMMER

40 BEAUTY-OUS BALM

Heaven Scent

Your chosen scent says a lot about you — it's an outward expression of the inner you. From the confidence of Orientals to the playfulness of florals, every perfume tells a powerful personal story.

So what better way to express the true you than by boiling and bubbling a scent of your very own? Turning your basement into a personal *parfumerie* is easier than you think. Here are a few fragrances we love, but feel free to fashion your own. These scents are strong, so just a dab will do!

grab:

* 100-PROOF VODKA (DON'T JUST BUST INTO THE LIQUOR CABINET — ASK YOUR PARENTS FIRST!) DO NOT SUBSTITUTE RUBBING ALCOHOL.

* ESSENTIAL AND FRAGRANCE OILS

* A MEASURING SPOON

* A NARROW FUNNEL FOR FILLING BOTTLES

* EYE DROPPERS

* A GLASS ROD FOR STIRRING

here's how:

* Sterilize bottles by boiling 10 minutes in hot water.

* Fill a small glass bottle with 1/2 teaspoon vodka.

* Add essential oils one at a time, in the order given; swirl the brew after adding each one.

Red Moon

6 drops essential oil of bergamot
16 drops tuberose fragrance oil
4 drops essential oil of ylang-ylang
6 drops gardenia fragrance oil
8 drops essential oil of sandalwood

Bali High

12 drops gardenia fragrance oil
6 drops jasmine fragrance oil
6 drops essential oil of bois de rose
6 drops amber fragrance oil

Really Rosy

6 drops essential oil of rose
3 drops essential oil of geranium
8 drops essential oil of sandalwood
2 drops essential oil of rosewood

Bottle It Up!

Glam gals know the panache of perfume is equal parts scent and sensational bottle. So get creative when decorating your containers. Comb flea markets, yard sales, and Grandma's attic for vintage bottles and vials. Be on the lookout for colorful glass, interesting shapes, funky gems, and jewels for decorating. Make a simple bottle snazzy with ribbons, lace, or dried flowers. And for an extra-posh touch, glue a trinket or two on top.

Body Art

Belly Burst

Belly buttons are beautiful, and showing yours off spells confidence! Here's a belly embellishment that doesn't require piercing or permanent tattooing.

grab:
* A kohl pencil
* A thin paintbrush
* Body paint
* Baby powder

here's how:
* Sketch a sunburst outline onto your tummy with kohl pencil. Go swirly, soft, or spiky — whatever befits your belly.
* Use a single color of body paint for the outline. With a paintbrush, fill in the fiery burst with a contrasting color or two.
* Powder lightly with baby powder to set the paint. (No worries, Mom, body paint washes off with soap and water.)

Bindi Queen

Bindis are body adornments borrowed from traditional Hindu style. Used as decoration, they lend an exotic element to the body. Add a sarong and you've got Eastern-inspired glam.

grab:
* Body paint (two colors)
* A thin paintbrush
* Bindis (find them in Indian fashion/food bazaars, ethnic boutiques, or accessory shops)
* Eyelash glue (used for attaching fake eyelashes)

here's how:
* Paint a center dot on your forehead, just above your eyebrow line. A pencil eraser is about the right size.
* In a contrasting color, paint a row of tiny dots to the left and right of the center circle. Your lines should curve upwards slightly in the middle.
* Attach a bindi to the central dot using eyelash glue. If it already has adhesive, just press on.
* Other ideas: Create an armband or anklet of tiny dots, with a bindi in the center. Or paste a single jewel on your cheek, forehead, or ankle.

From the body beading of Masai tribes to the henna-stained hands of Morocco, artful body adornment has been practiced since ancient times. And today, these age-old arts have become the most au courant of beauty trends. Add some international flair to your look with these glam ideas from around the globe.

orient express

Chinese characters can express our strongest emotions — love, joy, desire, envy, in a single symbol. Paint them on as temporary tattoos and say a lot in very few strokes.

grab:

* Body or henna ink   * A kohl pencil   * A thin paintbrush
* A book of Chinese characters

here's how:

* Pick out a character or symbol.
* Sketch the symbol with kohl pencil onto your ankle, arm, shoulder, belly, or back.
* Darken the lines with paint, using a thin brush.

幸 友

LUCKY FRIEND

Bandy-About Babe

Armbands are a strong sexy look for any arm. Bands can be painted on with henna ink, body paint, or eyeliner. Black or single-colored bands are your best bet — go with a shade that will stand out against your skin.

grab:

* A kohl pencil   * String or elastic band
* A thin paintbrush   * Baby powder
* Liquid eyeliner, henna ink, or body paint
* A friend to help you — this is a must!

here's how:

* Tie string or elastic around your arm to help make a straight band.
* Sketch a wavy center line with kohl pencil.
* Thicken the line with liquid eyeliner or henna.
* Add curlicues, dots, and dashes around the center line to fill out your band.
* Dust with baby powder to set.

Faux Moles

We'll never really know if Cindy Crawford's mole is faux or real. Or how it is that so many hip hot models just happen to have a beautiful brown one right above their upper lip. Here's how you can take fate (and face) into your own hands and make a mole of your very own. The beauty of this mark is that you can move it, change it, or chuck it whenever you please.

grab:

* A PILE OF FASHION MAGS

* A BLACK OR BROWN EYELINER PENCIL

here's how:

* Where to put your mole is up to you. Maybe above your lip, or on your cheek, or near your bellybutton for bikini sunbathing, or ... For inspiration, flip through fashion mags and find one on a model you think looks great.

* Draw the dot lightly at first. If you like the effect, darken and enlarge as you like.

which is worse?

* A UNIBROW OR A MUSTACHE?

* NO TOENAILS OR NO FINGERNAILS?

* LIPSTICK ON YOUR TEETH OR LUNCH IN YOUR TEETH?

* ACNE OR BACK-NE?

* NOSE HAIR OR CHIN HAIR?

* TOE CHEESE OR BELLY BUTTON LINT?

Shimmer Glimmer

Give a little kid some glitter, and the canister (enough for dozens of art projects) inevitably returns empty. There's something magical about its shimmer and shine that makes you want to cover every conceivable surface with it. And glam gals are no different. The more the better, as far as we're concerned! Here's how to sparkle from head-to-toe ...

grab:

* CRAFT GLITTER IN VARIOUS COLORS, SIZES, AND PATTERNS

* YOUR BASIC PRIMPING PRODUCTS — LOTION, HAIR GEL, VASELINE, NAIL POLISH, ETC.

know-it-all

The earliest film starlets wore blue lipstick to look glamorous in black-and-white.

here's how:

* Hair: Sprinkle some glitter on your hairbrush as you untangle your tresses. Or mix a bit into hair mousse or gel.

* Body: Put a dab of vaseline in your hand, and then add a dash of glitter. Rub in where you want shine. (Arms, shoulders, and collarbones are all choice spots.)

* Nails: Sprinkle some red glitter into your plain-Jane clear polish. Other combos to try: silver in red polish; green glitter in pink (Is it ultra-preppy or punk? You decide.)

* Cheeks: Dip your finger in lotion, and then in the glitter pot. Rub the colorful blend over the apples of your cheeks.

Beauty-ous Balm

Lips are for kissing — every GlamGirl knows that! And what better way to keep lips super-smoochable than with lip balm you make yourself? Whether your puckering preference is soft and supple or shiny and shimmery, here's how to get a perfect pout.

grab:

* A GLASS MEASURING CUP (WITH POURING SPOUT)

* A MEDIUM PAN

* DISPOSABLE DROPPERS (CHECK EYE/EAR OR BABY SECTION OF THE DRUGSTORE)

* POPSICLE STICKS (FOR STIRRING)

* 2 OR 3 SMALL ROUND PLASTIC OR GLASS CONTAINERS WITH LIDS

recipe:

* 1 1/2 TEASPOONS WHITE BEESWAX (OFTEN COMES IN PELLET FORM)

* 2 TEASPOONS COCOA BUTTER

* 2 TEASPOONS SHEA BUTTER

* 2 1/2 TEASPOONS SWEET ALMOND OIL

* 3 DROPS VITAMIN E OIL

* DRUGSTORE LIPSTICK

* SEVERAL DROPS FLAVORED OIL — PICK YOUR FAVE!

here's how:

✳ Create your own double boiler by placing a glass measuring cup in a pan filled with about 1 inch of water; put pan over low heat.

✳ Add the beeswax to the measuring cup and melt. (Don't overheat — it will get grainy.)

✳ Add the cocoa butter, shea butter, and sweet almond oil, and melt.

✳ Add the vitamin E oil, stirring frequently with a popsicle stick.

✳ Color your lip balm by shaving in a few tiny pieces of a cheap drugstore lipstick.

✳ Stir with a popsicle stick.

✳ Remove cup from the stove and pour balm into small containers.

✳ Use a dropper to add flavor oil last, several drops in each container.

✳ Stir quickly before the balm starts to harden.

Save face

Lipstick broken in bits? Scoop the broken bits into a small microwave-safe jar or an empty microwave pillbox. Microwave about 20 seconds. Apply with your finger or a lipbrush.

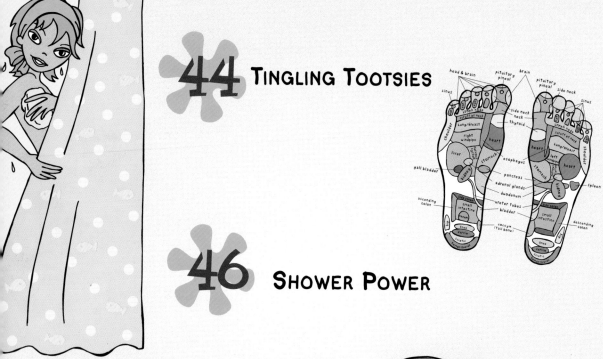

Tingling Tootsies

Treat your feet right with some minty-fresh pampering. What a breath mint does for your mouth, this decadent recipe will do for your feet: invigorate, revitalize, refresh.

grab:

* 1 TABLESPOON ALMOND OIL

* 1 TABLESPOON OLIVE OIL

* 1 TEASPOON WHEAT GERM OIL

* 12 DROPS EUCALYPTUS ESSENTIAL OR FRAGRANCE OIL, OR PEPPERMINT OIL

here's how:

* Combine ingredients in a jar or small dish and stir well.

* To use, get a friend to rub the treatment onto your feet and heels.

* Store in a cool dry place.

Knead Your Feet

Reflexology isn't just simple foot massage; practitioners believe that the foot is the control board to the entire body, with certain pressure points corresponding to various parts of the body. Headaches, a stuffy head and nose, and even cramps can all be pinpointed. Grab a clean-footed friend and take turns kneading each other's tootsies. Here's a map of the foot, with some key body parts matched up:

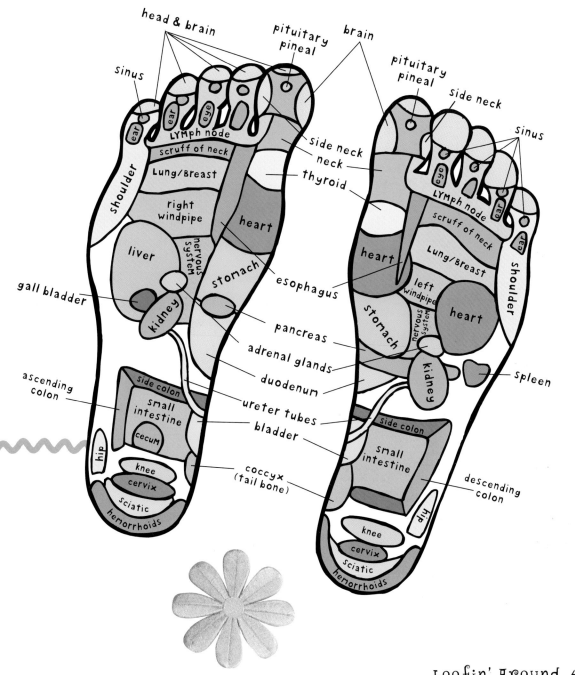

Shower Power

Rev Up

Who needs coffee when you can add zing to your morning routine with a refreshing splash? This one is sure to get you singing at the top of your lungs.

* **TIME OF DAY:** early morning, post nap
* **DURATION:** 15 minutes
* **RECOMMENDED SOUNDTRACK:** fire up Madonna, Whitney, or Mariah (the Divas will wake you up!)
* **PERFECT PRODUCTS:** citrus-scented soap to awaken your senses; tingling shampoo; creamy conditioner for maximum moisture
* **TAKE TIME TO:** exfoliate and stimulate your feet with a pumice stone or loofah

Pre-Party Prep

This party starts before the guests arrive. Get in a festive frame of mind with this wet and wild wash.

* **TIME OF DAY:** early evening
* **DURATION:** 30+ minutes
* **RECOMMENDED SOUNDTRACK:** get psyched with some pumping techno, some sultry soul, or that hot new hip-hop album
* **PERFECT PRODUCTS:** a good loofah to make your skin shine; vanilla-scented body wash; body-adding protein-enriched shampoo
* **TAKE TIME TO:** do a deep conditioning mask for healthy glowing complexion

Every shower you take is different — depending on your mood or the day's plans. Sometimes you need to decompress; sometimes you need to get ready to dress to impress. Pick your pleasure, draw the curtain, and soap up.

Stressed out

Take your troubles to the waters. There's nothing like drumming droplets and soothing scents to chill out your mood.

* **TIME OF DAY:** before bedtime, after a long day at school
* **DURATION:** 10–30 minutes (or as long as it takes to unwind …)
* **RECOMMENDED SOUNDTRACK:** try soothing mellow tunes from Joni Mitchell, Enya, or Sarah McLachlan
* **PERFECT PRODUCTS:** lavender oil to relax you; chamomile soap is soothing
* **TAKE TIME TO:** use a self-heating hair potion, or loofah your feet

Love Struck

Whether your crush finally called or cupid hasn't stopped on your corner, you can lather up some love in this homemade romance ritual. You'll emerge starry-eyed and sparkling clean.

* **TIME OF DAY:** anytime that lovin' feeling strikes!
* **DURATION:** 20–60 minutes
* **RECOMMENDED SOUNDTRACK:** groove to the classic croonings of Sade, your favorite boy band, or some love songs by Marvin Gaye
* **PERFECT PRODUCTS:** rose-scented body oil; a glittery body wash
* **TAKE TIME TO:** shave your legs with extra-rich cream for a really close shave

Big Night Beauty

Okay, tonight's the night. The big date. The party of the year. The prom. Whatever the occasion, get your face to glow with this 3-step beauty regime: steam, mask, splash. The steam clears pores, increases blood flow, and moisturizes; the mask tightens and revitalizes tired skin; the splash refreshes and preps for makeup. Ready, set, glam!

Steam Queen

grab:

4 DRIED BAY LEAVES

1 TABLESPOON DRIED CHAMOMILE FLOWERS

1 TABLESPOON DRIED ROSEMARY

1 HANDFUL FRESH OR DRIED ROSE PETALS

4 CUPS BOILING WATER

BATH TOWEL

here's how:

* Put bay leaves, chamomile flowers, rosemary, and rose petals in a large bowl.

* Pour boiling water over herbs

* Put your face about 12 inches above the bowl, covering your head with a towel to form a tent.

* Steam for 5–10 minutes and listen to soothing tunes while you soak up the vapors.

* Splash your face with cool water.

Whitewash

grab:

1 EGG WHITE

here's how:

* Beat egg white in a small bowl.

* Using your fingers, apply wash to your face, especially to the T-zone.

* Leave on for about 15 minutes.

* Rinse well with warm water, then follow with a splash of cool water. Pat dry.

cool-as-a-cuke splash

grab:

1/2 CUCUMBER

1/4 CUP WATER

4 FRESH MINT LEAVES

1 SHEET CHEESECLOTH OR 1 PAPER COFFEE FILTER

know-it-all

In Elizabethan England, women slept with slices of raw beef on their faces to get rid of wrinkles!

here's how:

* Peel and slice half a cucumber (save the other half for tonight's salad).

* Mix remaining cuke and water in a blender until the cucumber is smooth.

* Add the mint leaves to the mixture. Blend until smooth.

* Strain mixture through cheesecloth or coffee filter into a bowl or jar.

* Splash the cuke juice on your face or apply with a cotton ball. Relax and recline with a cucumber slice over each eye.

Pantry Pampering

Fresh-Squeezed Face (smooths out blotchy skin)

* 1 EGG WHITE

* 1 TEASPOON FROZEN ORANGE JUICE CONCENTRATE

* 1 TEASPOON LEMON JUICE (USE REAL OR BOTTLED)

* Beat egg white in a small bowl.

* Whisk in orange juice concentrate and lemon juice.

* Apply to face with fingers or cotton ball.

* Leave on for 20 minutes.

* Rinse well with warm water, then follow with a splash of cool water.

Pooh Pampering (great for blemishes)

* 1 EGG

* 1 TABLESPOON WHOLE MILK

* 1 TABLESPOON HONEY

* Mix all the ingredients together in a small bowl.

* Let mixture come to room temperature.

* Apply to your face and leave on for 20 minutes or until hardened.

* Rinse well with warm water, then follow with a splash of cool water.

Bet you didn't know that everything you need to get gorgeous is right in your pantry. Simple wholesome ingredients like honey, oatmeal, eggs, and milk make great meals — but they're also terrific for your skin and hair! Raid the fridge and try these easy down-home recipes.

Morning Glory

✱ 2 TABLESPOONS PLAIN YOGURT

✱ 1 TABLESPOON UNCOOKED OATMEAL

✱ 1 TABLESPOON CORNMEAL

Mix all ingredients together in a small bowl.

✱ Let mixture come to room temperature.

✱ Apply to face (or body) with a circular massaging motion.
Leave for 5–10 minutes.

✱ Rinse well with warm water, then follow with a splash of cool water.

carbo-load

✱ 1 CUP UNCOOKED OATMEAL

✱ 1 CUP BRAN

✱ 1/4 CUP ALMOND MEAL

✱ 1 SMALL MUSLIN OR COTTON BAG

✱ Mix all the ingredients together.

✱ Place in the bag.

✱ While you fill the bath, place the bag in the water to soak.

✱ Dive right in — you can even use the bag as a scrub cloth while you bathe.

Bombs Away

Bath bubbles are so done. Try this recipe for a *fizzing* bath bomb and relax your cares away in *fragrant* soothing bliss. Wrap the bombs up in cellophane and tie with a colorful ribbon to make a great *gift* for friends and teachers.

grab:

* 1/4 CUP BAKING SODA

* 2 TABLESPOONS CORNSTARCH

* 2 TABLESPOONS CITRIC ACID

* 1 TABLESPOON COCONUT, ALMOND, AVOCADO OR APRICOT KERNEL OIL

* 1/2 TABLESPOON WATER

* 3–6 DROPS LIQUID COLORANT (OPTIONAL)

* 1/4 TEASPOON FRAGRANCE OIL OR ESSENTIAL OIL OF YOUR CHOICE (TRY PEPPERMINT, EUCALYPTUS, OR VANILLA) (OPTIONAL)

here's how:

* Put baking soda, corn starch, and citric acid into a bowl and mix well.

* In a separate bowl, mix the oil, water, fragrance, and colorant.

* Slowly add the oil mixture to the dry ingredients and blend well.

* Shape the dough into about golf-ball sized globes and place on waxed paper.

* Let harden on waxed paper for 2–3 hours; reshape if needed.

* Continue to let the balls harden for 24-48 hours.

* Store in a closed container.

* Use 1–3 bath bombs in warm bath water for a fantastic fizzy treat!

Bad Girls' French Manicure

Sure, French manicures are nice. They're a classic: understated, neat, and simple. But to make your 10 digits really stand out and show some style, try this racy version of that plain-Jane manicure.

grab:

* CLEAR POLISH

* 2 DARK BUT CONTRASTING NAIL COLORS

here's how:

* Start with clean polish-free nails.

* Apply a light basecoat of clear polish, followed by a coat of blue polish (or whatever color you choose).

* As it dries, apply another coat (for maximum color saturation).

* Now, here's the tricky (but fun) part. Take your second shade, and gently swipe a swath of color along the top edge of your nail.

* Each edge should look like a sliver — too much, it may drip; too little, it may smudge.

Save face

Avoid one more wrecked manicure. Take nonstick cooking spray and give your fingers or toes a once-over.

steppin' out

Glam
Dare-a-Day Wheel

"i dare you" — three tiny words that produce action when said together! What better way to fire up your glam factor — fast — than with daily dares dished out by your friends. Here, you and your gang invent style challenges for one another to follow. Everyone makes a spinning wheel of her own, writes the group's dares on it, and then spins to see where the fashion fortunes fall! Do you dare?

we dare you

* Wear something strapless.

* Wear something backless.

* Wear pj bottoms as pants.

* Put on an animal print and prowl about.

* Wear fake eyelashes — and flirt!

* Wear red shoes — you're not in Kansas anymore.

* Part your hair in the middle for the day.

* Wear something camo with stripes.

* Wear a cami instead of a bra.

* Wear a little lace with something black.

* Bare some belly button with low-rise pants and a short shirt.

* Wear patent leather shoes with blue jeans.

* Wear something with fringe.

grab:

* A 12 x 12-INCH PIECE OF CARDBOARD OR HEAVY POSTER BOARD

* COLORED MARKERS

* CONSTRUCTION PAPER

* A RULER

* A SPINNER (CHECK CRAFT STORES, OR BORROW FROM AN OLD BOARD GAME)

dare-a-day wheel

TOTALLY 80S
STRAPLESS
PJS TO SCHOOL
LACE WITH BLACK
INSIDE-OUT CLOTHES
FRINGE
CHECKERS & STRIPES
BARE BELLY
RED SHOES
BACKLESS
ALL ORANGE

here's how:

* Sit around with your girl gang and create your list of glam dares. The idea is to force each other out of the fashion comfort zone.

* Check out the previous page for some dares to give you ideas. Use these if you like, but come up with your own, too. Half the fun is creating the challenges — you know how to push each other's buttons best!

* Make your wheel: Draw a large circle on the cardboard — stop about 1 inch from the edge. Cover with colorful construction paper. Use a ruler to divide your circle into 16 equal-sized pie pieces. Punch a hole in the center and attach the spinner.

* Decide on the best dares as a group and write them into the sections of your wheel. Pick a variety — some about clothes, makeup, hair, etc.

* Agree to the rules you'll play by. Is there a prize for the girl that dares to do all? Do you spin every day for a week, or only on Fridays?

Remember, no guts, no glory, no glamour!

Bye, bye boring: Everyday Glam

Why be boring if you can be dazzling? Back-to-basics may have its moment, but sometimes you gotta pull out all the stops. Here are four glam makeovers for ordinary moments:

transform	into	must-haves	expressions
A DRAB DRIVE HOME FROM SCHOOL	A GLAM GET-AWAY	LONG SCARF (FOR WHIPPING NONCHALANTLY AROUND NECK), EXAGGERATED WAVE, SUNGLASSES, ENGINE THAT REVS	LATER DAHHHLINNNNNGGG!
A NIGHT OF HOMEWORK	A GIRLY GAB SESSION	SOME REALLY JUICY GOSSIP, A RECENT ENCOUNTER WITH A NEW CRUSH, LOUD TUNES TO DROWN OUT LAUGHTER, MUNCHIES	I SWORE I WOULDN'T TELL ANYONE, BUT IF YOU SWEAR TO SAY NOTHING …
A GRANOLA BAR BEFORE SCHOOL	A CLASSY BREAKFAST	CHAMPAGNE FLUTES FOR OJ, ORANGE MARMALADE FOR TOAST, BACH IN THE BACKGROUND, ARTSY MAGS.	THIS JAM IS JUST DIVINE!
FRIDAY NIGHT VIDEOS AT HOME	A SILVER-SCREEN EXTRAVAGANZA	A FILM STARRING AUDREY HEPBURN OR GRACE KELLY, CHOCOLATE KISSES IN A TINY SILVER DISH, A SILKY KIMONO AND HEELED SLIPPERS	*BREAKFAST AT TIFFANY'S* IS WHAT MOVIES WERE MADE TO BE

Mirror, Mirror on the Wall

Sometimes, how you feel about yourself is as simple as what you see. Remake your mirror to reflect the ~~attitude~~ you want to project. Feisty, fun, poetic, or pensive — your looking glass can be whatever you want. Start every day with a look into a personalized mirror.

grab:

* SCISSORS
* MAGAZINES
* DRIED FLOWERS
* PHOTOS
* DOUBLE-SIDED TAPE OR THUMBTACKS
* COLORED PENCILS, MARKERS, AND CONSTRUCTION PAPER
* BEADS, FELT, AND OTHER DECORATIONS

here's how:

* If you are a budding writer, write your favorite quotes around your mirror's border.
* Paste favorite shots of friends and family around your mirror. (Feel free to cut out your ex's head from old pictures!)
* Dried roses give a romantic feminine feel.
* Feeling frisky? Pucker up and add a few blood-red lipstick kisses to the mirror.
* Star struck? Clip pictures of your latest on-screen obsessions.

What Signals Are You Sending?

While you make like you're having fun, those crossed arms and stiff upper body say otherwise. Body language speaks louder than words — and fools no one. What's your posture pointing to?

1 A cute new guy shows up at school. You:

A. Sit down next to him at lunch and strike up a conversation.

B. Look him up and down from across the hall, wondering when he'll notice you.

C. Don't take much notice — what's he got going besides cute?

D. Walk right by him, keeping your head to the ground. After all, what would he want with you anyway?

2 You're meeting friends at a party, but when you walk in you don't see anyone you know. You:

A. Ditch your coat, grab a drink, and start chatting.

B. Stand by the wall with your arms crossed, checking out the scene. Someone will recognize you soon.

C. Go straight to the stereo area and start talking music with whoever's spinning CDs.

D. Back out the door and wait on the walk for someone you know.

Mostly Ds: You're uncomfortable in your own skin, and it shows. You figure it's better to stick to the sidelines than risk doing something stupid in the spotlight. Try taking a few more chances and the rewards will be well worth it!

Mostly Cs: You march to the beat of your own drum. You've never put much stock in what others think, and aren't about to start. You're content to stand apart from the crowd — even if that means standing alone at times.

3

It's the first beach day of the year and you're looking pretty pale. You:

A. Jump into your bikini and spend the day soaking up rays.

B. Cluster closely with your girlfriends, quick to comment on other people's bathing suits and bodies.

C. Wear a one-piece, lather on the sunscreen, and get into a game of volleyball.

D. Head off to the beach, but skip swimming so you can keep your tee and shorts on.

4

You're waiting for the team roster to be posted. You:

A. Take a seat in the hall and gossip with others about the weekend.

B. Whisper with your friends (a little too loudly) about who will make it — and who won't.

C. Leave and check back later. The list isn't going anywhere.

D. Sit alone at the edge of the gym, arms crossed.

5

It's Halloween and there's a costume party at school. You:

A. Dress as a duck – and get into the spirit by clucking around and moving your arms.

B. Come in a group costume with your closest friends and spend the entire night in a tight circle, laughing among yourselves.

C. Skip the party and head to a scary movie with an old friend.

D. Skip the costume — who needs the embarrassment?

answers

Mostly As: Calm, cool, and collected. Your body says, "I like who I am — and I bet you will, too." Others are attracted to your ease, control, and sweat-free palms.

Mostly Bs: You have attitude – a bit more than you need. You look down your nose a little too far and have a way of making others feel two inches tall. Time to check what image you're projecting.

candid camera

Turn an ordinary Friday night with the girls into a glamorous fashion shoot. You'll have a blast — and some souvenirs from the fun for years to come.

grab:

* A COLORED OR PATTERNED SHEET

* YOUR HAIR AND MAKEUP BAG

* A PILE OF FUNKY CLOTHES AND SHOES

* A CAMERA AND FILM

here's how:

* Find a well-lighted place to do your shoot: a clean corner of your room or a nook in the basement.

* Hang the sheet on a wall to create a cool backdrop. The sheet will make the images really POP! in the picture.

* Pump up the music (whatever gets you in the mood to face the camera).

* Pair off with a pal for hair and makeup. You do her look; she does yours. Try that spiked look you saw in a magazine, overdo the glitter, and break all the rules. This is high fashion!

* Get dressed. Pair wacky platforms with an ugly old mini and a ripped sweatshirt for that street-glam look. Fishnets and an old prom dress would also look great.

* Check the light — try angling some watts toward the sheet so you pick up every last expression!

* Move, strut, strike a sultry pose, flip your hair back, and exaggerate every move you make.

* Say cheese and snap away!

Glam Slam Books

No matter how **hip** and happenin' you already are, everyone can use some candid style advice. And who better to offer **valuable** suggestions than your girlfriends? Serve up **tips** anonymously with these fun and frank slam books.

grab:

* A STACK OF 3 x 5 CARDS
* PENS OR PENCILS
* A HOLE PUNCH
* STRING OR RIBBON

here's how:

* Give everyone a handful of cards, each pre-labeled with a name on top.

* Grab a pen and start slamming — dish on your favorite things about each other's looks, closet contents, and everything in between. Be honest, but keep it kind!

* When you're done with each person's style profile, gather the cards and sort them by name.

* Punch a hole and secure with string and **voila** — a glamour manual from the people who know you best!

Here are some fun and provocative phrases to get the slamming started:

* Your worst fashion moment was…
* Your best fashion moment was…
* My favorite thing about your look is…
* If I were you, I'd consider changing…
* The best color for you is…
* The worst color for you is…
* If you were an animal, I think you'd be a…
* The item I most covet from your closet is…
* Your classic look consists of…